Copyright © 2003 by Lemniscaat b.v. Rotterdam
ISBN 1-93245-01-2
Originally published in The Netherlands
under the title *de gele ballon* by Lemniscaat b.v. Rotterdam
Printed and bound in Belgium
CIP data is available
First U.S. edition

the yellow balloon

CHARLOTTE DEMATONS

Front Street & Lemniscaat
Asheville, North Carolina